WALT DISNEY'S FAMOUS
SEVEN DWARFS

SNEEZY

BASHFUL

DOPEY

HERE ARE
THE SEVEN DWARFS

HAPPY

GRUMPY

SLEEPY

DOC

Grumpy tells the other Dwarfs something dreadful will happen soon. Do you remember how in the movie and in the story we are told that he has been warning them about this for several hundred years?

The Dwarfs discover Snow White, and Snow White discovers the Dwarfs. They are curious and Snow White is surprised. Imagine awakening and finding seven little men looking at you,

Grumpy says, "Get rid of her. Nothing good will come of it." But the
Dwarfs find out that Snow White can cook, and their hearts and stomachs
vote for her. Grumpy, too, learns to love Snow White.

Snow White makes them wash before eating. Here they are obeying her command. It is all very strange to them, for they have not washed for a very long time. But they find that soap and water are not half bad.

After supper there is great joy and merriment. What funny instruments they play! Grumpy is playing the piano. Doc, as usual, is the leader. Snow White watches and applauds. They are all very happy.

Then they dance. Grumpy is still sure that he does not approve. But he cannot stay out of all the fun. It is very late before the party is over. Snow White and the Dwarfs have become very good friends.

A great idea comes to the Dwarfs. They will make a gift for Snow White. They are now planning what it is to be.

They are busy building a bed for Snow White, each one happy in working out his part, when the birds and animals bring an alarm. There is danger for Snow White, the wicked Queen has appeared with the poisoned apple. They race to the rescue.

Alas! They are too late. Snow White lies there as if asleep, while they mourn for her. She will remain lifeless and still until the prince appears. When he does she will come to life and they will mount his horse together and travel to his home. But every spring Snow White and the prince will journey back and visit the home of the Seven Dwarfs.

The End